T0198563

The Pepa Bus

Leticia Roa Nixon (Ahdanah)

© 2020 Leticia Roa Nixon (Ahdanah). All rights reserved.

No part of this book may be reproduced, stored in
a retrieval system, or transmitted by any means
without the written permission of the author.

AuthorHouse™
1663 Liberty Drive
Bloomington, IN 47403
www.authorhouse.com
Phone: 1 (800) 839-8640

Because of the dynamic nature of the Internet, any web addresses or
links contained in this book may have changed since publication and may
no longer be valid. The views expressed in this work are solely those
of the author and do not necessarily reflect the views of the publisher,
and the publisher hereby disclaims any responsibility for them.

Any people depicted in stock imagery provided by Getty Images are models,
and such images are being used for illustrative purposes only.
Certain stock imagery © Getty Images.

This book is printed on acid-free paper.

ISBN: 978-1-7283-4762-2 (sc)
ISBN: 978-1-7283-4763-9 (e)

Library of Congress Control Number: 2020903485

Print information available on the last page.

Published by AuthorHouse 02/21/2020

author HOUSE®

Dedication

To Sharon C. Ortiz-Belpre (September 19, 1971-April 16, 2014), daughter of Don Domingo, who inspired this book.

© Can Stock Photo Inc/colematt

Sharon rubbed her eyes awake, the alarm clock's loud ring still piercing in her ears and resounding in her head. She plopped back down in her warm bed for a couple of minutes. It was three in the morning.

Sharon looked through the small window and greeted the stars with a lively, "Buenos días."

She felt the gentle breeze of the summer morning as she quickly dressed. Today she'll go with her father, Don Domingo, to pick the juicy, navy-blue blueberries in a nearby state farm.

Sharon stuffed a towel, a big straw hat, a large empty cookie can with a strapped belt, a large bottle of water, and a sandwich in her bag.

© Can Stock Photo Inc/colematt

She rushed down the steps and into the narrow street. Her father was waiting for her in a beat-up jalopy of a yellow school bus. The neighbors called it The Pepa Bus. Sharon nestled in the first row, right behind her father's seat.

© Can Stock Photo Inc/srsallay

Don Domingo pulled off and yelled with his husky voice, "Laaaaa Peeeeppaaaaaa!" alerting the neighbors that he was en route to the blueberry farm.

It reminded Sharon of a rooster singing a wake-up call early in the morning.

He stopped at four corners on his daily route. Men, women and children were waiting for The Pepa Bus in the wee hours of the morning when it was still dark and chilly. Some stood in front of the closed "bodega" shivering. Many of them came from small row houses around the corner.

© Can Stock Photo Inc/curvabezier

"Laaaaa Peeeeppaaaaaa!" Don Domingo yelled again at his last stop before taking the highway that would take them to the Garden State.

The Pepa Bus was filled up except for the seat next to Sharon.

She looked through the window and saw her friend.

"Daddy," pleaded Sharon, "there's Angel running down the street. Stop!"

© Can Stock Photo Inc/colematt

The lanky long-haired teenager climbed quickly into The Pepa Bus and sat next to her.

© Can Stock Photo Inc/benchart

Yesterday he was late and had to catch a different bus that took him to a tomato farm instead of the usual blueberry field.

Sharon prided herself to be a "pepera," a blueberry picker. She remembered Angel's first time in the fields -- he didn't know squat about picking blueberries.

She shared her technique with Angel on how to fill the crates quickly. "The trick is to stand underneath the highbush tree, and rake the blueberries real fast with your fingers," she told him many times.

Sharon smiled broadly and happily to help Angel. She looked up to him as the older brother she didn't have.

Some of the pickers were having breakfast; bread rolls with hot coffee. Other pickers were napping.

"We're here!" announced Don Domingo after the long ride. It was six o'clock in the morning. He greeted the foreman, Mr. Jones, at the entrance gate of the farm. He was a tall with a muscled body and a face with chiseled features. Sharon had never seen him smile.

Mr. Jones instructed the new pickers not to jump over the ropes, which meant they had to stay in the same row of blueberry bushes they started in. He would assign the rows for the day to each picker.

Sharon and Angel stared at the blueberry fields with lots and lots of rows.

Angel had guessed that there were at least twenty bushes in each row. The row of bushes was probably about two city blocks long when they were all lined up. They looked down the rows and saw arches of blueberry bushes.

Sharon and Angel knew that blueberries don't actually grow on trees, but in bushes. Fortunately, the tall bushes tend to bend over with the weight of the blueberries and Sharon and Angel were ready to start picking.

© Can Stock Photo Inc/izakowski

Mr. Jones assigned Sharon and Angel to the same row. That meant they would work side by side on the same row, each plucking the fruit from the highbushes.

Soon they started to rake the ripe blueberries.

"Remember Angel, no green or orange blueberries," said Sharon.

"Fine with me," replied Angel as he ran his fingers through the bush to pluck the navy-blueberries.

Sharon remembered how her father had taught her everything. Blueberries that were reddish or orange were not ripe and should not be picked off the bush.

She was pretty fast. Her little fingers sensed which ones were not ripe and left the red ones to stay on the bush, since with time they will ripen.

Sharon preferred to wear the large cookie can around her, and where she placed the blueberries. Don Domingo had cut two holes into it to thread through her belt to be tied around her waist.

The blueberries fell into her can creating a harmony that sounded like rain drops on a tin roof.

Once she filled her can, she emptied it on the crates along the row of blueberry bushes. Angel would come to pick them up and take them to a truck that would come from the main road. The truck attendant gave you a ticket for every crate you turned in.

Angel came back to the spot in the row where Sharon was standing and told her, "Stash these tickets very carefully in your pocket, I'll get three more empty crates."

Angel watched over Sharon so other pickers wouldn't steal her crates filled with the ripe blueberries.

At noon, Sharon wrapped a towel around her forehead and covered her head with a wide straw hat. "It's hot today," Sharon said in a loud voice, "and I mean a very hot day. I am so glad I wore a hat that can protect me from the scorching sun." She had been plucking blueberries without a break for six hours under the bright sun.

It was lunch time. The smell of fried chicken wafted through the hot air.

"Mmm, it smells delicious. I'm going to buy me some chicken and fries", Angel declared. "Do you want to come?" he asked Sharon.

"Not now, I'll catch up with you soon!" she replied encouraging him to go to the food truck.

© Can Stock Photo Inc/mcherevan

By the time they broke for lunch, Sharon and Angel had worked up an appetite and were dehydrated.

The sweltering heat made her more tired and thirsty, but she needed more tickets to cash in at the end of the day. Suddenly, the blueberries in her hands looked so good. "Just this time," she said to herself, trying to convince herself it was a good idea.

Sharon had just popped a handful of blueberries into her mouth when she saw the tall and iron-muscle foreman standing in front of her. She gasped when she knew she was caught red-handed.

© Can Stock Photo Inc/krisdog

"Now, you know I will report it to your father and the farm owner. These blueberries don't belong to you," he reprimanded her sternly.

Sharon stood there feeling like her stomach had been punched, her eyes watering and her cheeks feeling like hot coals on her face. The blueberries were still in her mouth and slowly going down her throat. She was so afraid her body started shaking.

Angel came running up to them when he saw Sharon trembling and that she had been pulled out the row of highbush blueberries by the foreman.

© Can Stock Photo Inc/colematt

"Mr. Jones is there anything I can do to help out?" he asked looking at him in the eye.

"Well, I don't know. I saw Sharon eating blueberries she had just picked. I'm going to tell the farmer," he retorted.

"May I pay for the blueberries she ate to make up for it? I'm sure she won't do it again," pleaded Angel.

"You really care a lot for her. And she's one of the best blueberry pickers we have, you know. Well, I think it is a fair deal and I accept it," agreed the foreman.

Sharon rushed into Angel's arms and buried her head in his chest crying with relief.

"Hey, it's OK now. Come and I'll treat you to a chicken sandwich, it's really yummy!"

"Thank you so much Angel," Sharon said between sobs.

© Can Stock Photo Inc/Kakigori

Sharon wiped her tears with her hand, straightened her straw hat and walked to the food truck holding Angel's arm. Soon it was time to go back to their assigned row and continue picking.

"The heat is so much different than what I recall when I lived in Puerto Rico," Angel told Sharon. "In Puerto Rico, I could always find me a palm tree, coco tree, or banana tree to hide from the scorching sun."

"Well here, I swear if you could put an egg on my head it would fry for sure," Sharon joked.

The afternoon blueberry picking hours went faster after lunch time. Sharon was happy again and whistled as she quickly picked the plump, juicy blueberries.

She then took her tickets to be cashed.

On her way back to the row, Sharon heard her father's voice, "Time to board the bus!!!" It was five o'clock in the afternoon. When Sharon was on her way to The Pepa Bus, she saw Mr. Jones talking with her father. *I wonder if he already told him about me eating the blueberries*, thought Sharon.

Angel looked in the same direction and hurried to be at Sharon's side to get on the bus together.

"Go ahead, Angel," said Don Domingo.

Then the husky driver put an arm around Sharon and whispered in her ear, "My little daughter, you had a hard lesson today, but it's over now, let's go home." Don Domingo believed in Sharon, how hard-working she was, and he would make sure that nothing and no one would hurt her.

© Can Stock Photo Inc/colematt

Sharon looked at her Dad's suntanned face, his eyes shining like the bright sun and his broad smile. She hugged him and then climbed up to take her seat next to Angel.

© Can Stock Photo Inc/bonairina

The Pepa Bus went jalopy, jalopy, jalopy away with the blueberry pickers. Sharon and Angel looked through the window at the trees and houses, cows, and rolls and rolls of various fruits and vegetables and other "peperos" picking away. They enjoyed watching the beauty of the sky. The beautiful Bald Eagles flying freely in the peaceful clear blue sky. Sharon admired the houses with white picket fences and swings in the front and back yards.

Stories were told by the older pickers about when they were growing up on the island and how they came to America.

© Can Stock Photo Inc/jpldesign

The young ones talked about how much more the tomato picking pays and how from the blueberry picking they could go to other farms to pick peaches.

Wow, that sounds like a promotion, it gives me hope to earn more money. Today blueberries, tomorrow tomatoes, and then who knows, thought Angel.

Sharon cuddled against Angel and fell asleep. She dreamed The Pepa Bus turned into a yellow three-story high house where the blueberry pickers lived happy as one strong and beautiful family. We, meaning the Puerto Ricans, Mexicans, Cubans, African Americans and some Koreans and Chinese that were part of the farming family and proudly accepted being known as the "Peperos".

Angel's gentle nudge woke her up. "We're back in the city, I'm getting off now. See you next time," he whispered.

Sharon yawned and muttered, "Till next time," as her eyes opened and saw her neighborhood once again. The rowhouses and "bodegas" rolled by as Don Domingo drove La Pepa Bus along the Avenue, and Sharon smiled as she saw her house in the distance.

© Can Stock Photo Inc/colematt

The End

© Can Stock Photo Inc/izakowski

Vocabulary

Bodega – popular term for grocery store

Buenos días - Good morning

Pepa – popular term for blueberry

Pepera – popular term female blueberry picker

Peperos – popular term for blueberry pickers

Printed in the United States
By Bookmasters